No Trouble at All

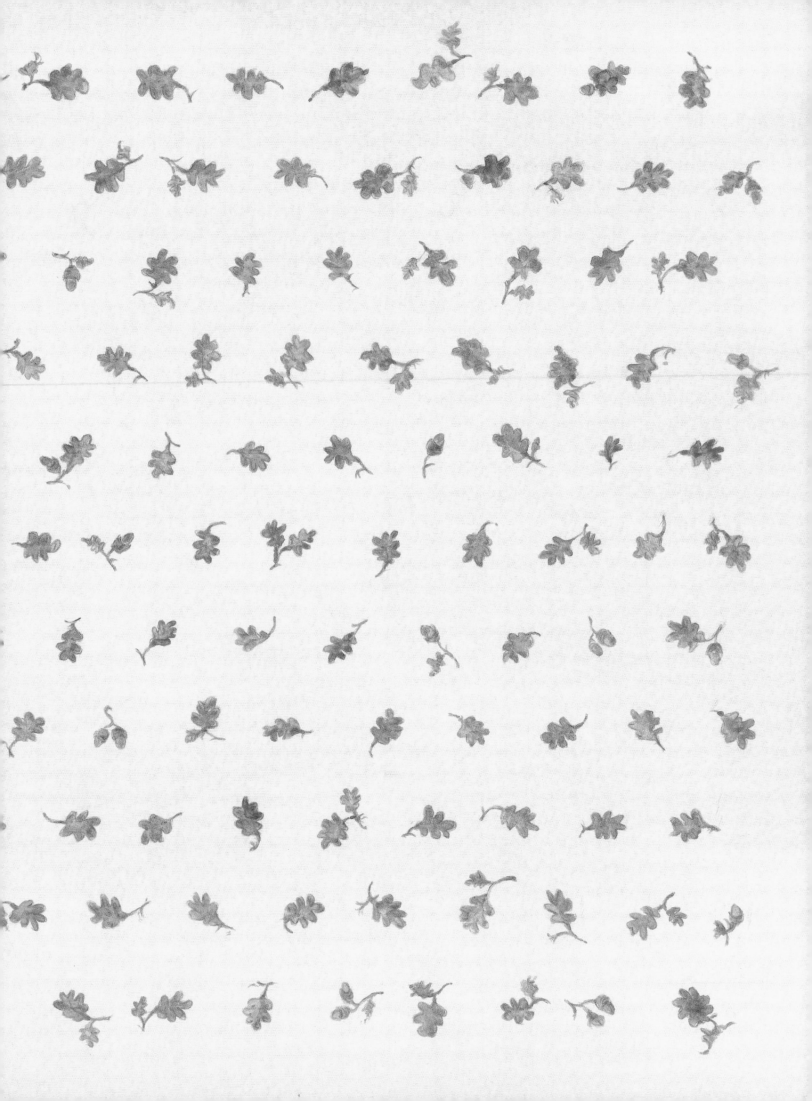

For Stephen and Liz Baird,
with many thanks – SG

For Paulina, Mary Elizabeth,
Dorothy and Valentina McNeill – ET

ISBN 0-439-73141-0

12 11 10 9 8 7 6 5 4 3 2   5 6 7 8 9 10/0

Printed in the U.S.A.   08

First Scholastic printing, February 2005

No Trouble at All

by Sally Grindley
illustrated by Eleanor Taylor

SCHOLASTIC INC.
New York Toronto London Auckland Sydney
Mexico City New Delhi Hong Kong Buenos Aires

Shhh! They're fast asleep.
Don't wake them up.

They're such good little bears when they come to stay.

I just have to say it's time
for bed, and off they go,
as good as gold.

When I was their age
I was full of mischief.

These old houses are full of strange noises.
I'd better just check those little bears
aren't frightened.

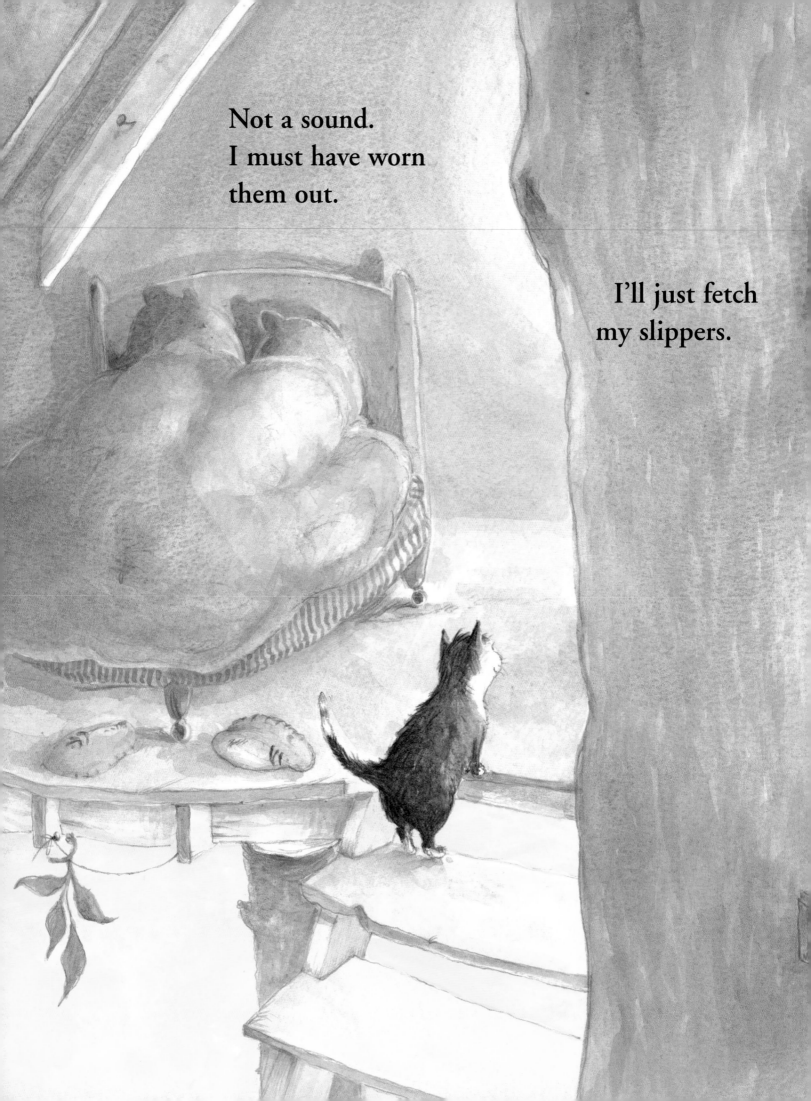

Not a sound.
I must have worn
them out.

I'll just fetch
my slippers.

Ah, here they are.

Their mother says those little bears can be very naughty. I'm sure that can't be true.

What was that?

I guess I didn't close the door
properly. Silly of me.

It's a beautiful night.
If it's sunny tomorrow
we'll all go for a picnic.

I'll just fetch
the picnic basket
from the shed.

Here we are. Tomorrow
I'll fill it with sandwiches
and cakes and chocolates and
drinks and off we'll go.

They deserve a treat, those little bears. They're absolutely no trouble.

No trouble at all.

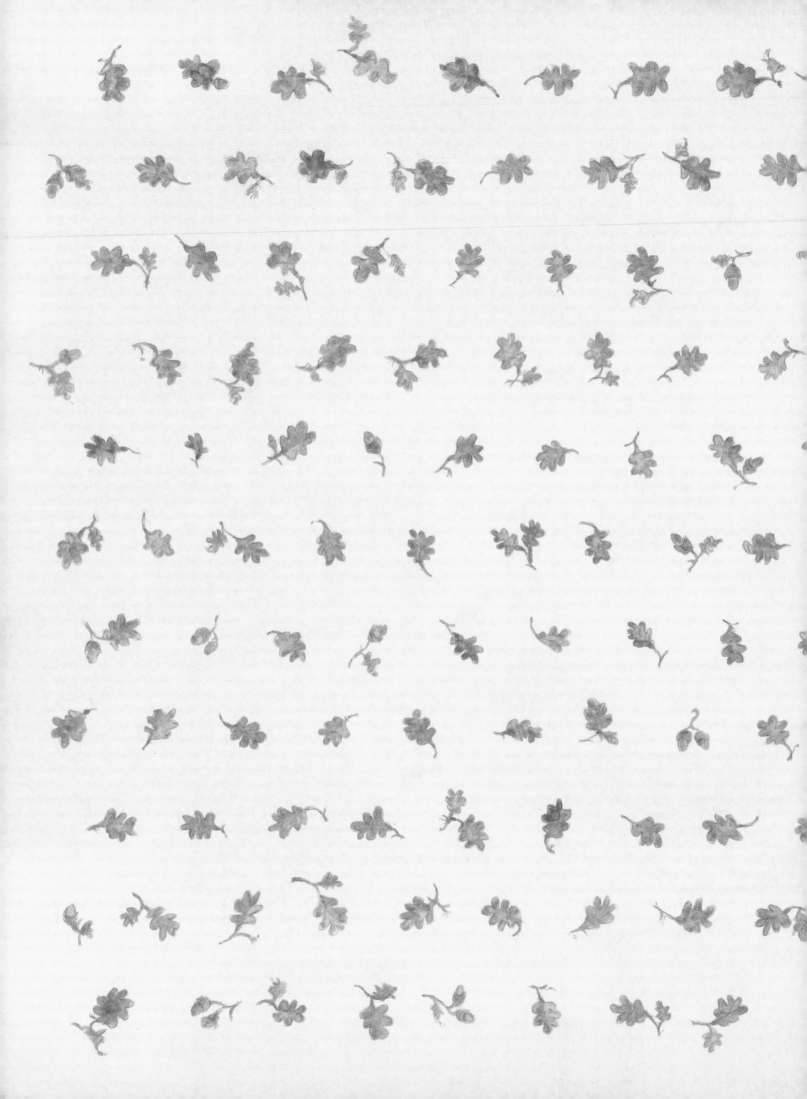